'A sensuous and strikingly visual story, this tale about motherhood is at once singular and universal. It taps into those equivocal feelings we all have about the conflicting burdens and joys of creating and supporting a tiny life, while showing us one woman's particular challenges. It is a ghost story which, even in these supposedly rational times, we completely fall into.'

—Julia Crouch

'Tara Gould knows an essential truth, that ghosts exist in the darkness of the mind. And that sometimes those ghosts can exit the mind and take up residence in the world. They need to be both real, and unreal, at the same time. It is a difficult task to pull off, and Gould tackles it superbly. This beguiling and unsettling story has a very powerful effect on the reader.'

—Jeff Noon

'An eerily evocative snapshot of a young woman possessed by her own lost history, *The Haunting of Strawberry Water* takes what should be the most secure of bonds, the relationship between mother and daughter, and transports it to a new and terrifying landscape of the uncanny.'

—Ian Breckon

'Elegant and profound, this is powerful nature writing as much as it is a compelling ghost story, and an expertly handled meditation on the prickly nature of intimate relationships.'

—Hannah Vincent

The Haunting of Strawberry Water

Tara
Gould

THE HAUNTING
OF STRAWBERRY
WATER

First published in 2020 by
Myriad Editions
www.myriadeditions.com

Myriad Editions
An imprint of New Internationalist Publications
The Old Music Hall, 106–108 Cowley Rd,
Oxford OX4 1JE

First printing
1 3 5 7 9 10 8 6 4 2

A CIP catalogue record for this book
is available from the British Library

ISBN (pbk): 978-1-912408-50-4
ISBN (ebk): 978-1-912408-51-1

Designed by WatchWord Editorial Services, London
Typeset in Dante by www.twenty-sixletters.com

Printed and bound in Great Britain
by CPI Group (UK) Ltd, Croydon CR0 4YY

For Karen,
who encouraged me to write this story

For most of my life, the only image I possessed of my mother was a shadowy, indistinct figure in an old Polaroid photograph.

She left when I was very small. I couldn't bring to mind the sound of her voice, or remember her face, but as a child I succeeded in constructing an imaginary substitute from the few anecdotal details I'd assembled. The Polaroid was a crucial component in my collection. To the casual observer, it would appear simply to be a family snapshot, generic and unremarkable—the colours are slightly muted, the clothes out of date. In it, I am being held on my father's knee, wearing a puffy yellow dress, in front of Strawberry Water, my childhood home.

I must be about a year old. My father is wearing a pale-blue, short-sleeved shirt and has wavy, shoulder-length hair, and we're sitting on the top of three whitewashed, wooden steps that lead to the front door of the bungalow. It's a bright spring day, the lawn is green and there are flowering shrubs in the beds, and crimson geraniums in terracotta pots. Behind us, the front door is open, and in contrast, the inside of the house is dark and colourless. There is an internal door to the right, which is ajar, and behind it stands a figure, a sliver of body, a sense of motion, as if the person lingering there is about to join us. All that's visible is a section of leg where the knee pushes forward, the point of a black, shiny shoe protruding at the base of the wooden door, and three slim fingers clutching the door half way up. The rest is simply the vague impression of the form and presence of a person. My mother.

As a child, I pestered my father for more photographs of her—pictures that showed her properly. I longed to see her face, its expression, the colour of her hair, the style of clothes she wore. But every time I asked my father, the question always elicited the same response: a swift, still silence would descend

2

upon him, making his usually animated body solid, and he would look away from me. Even as a child I knew he had his reasons. I never doubted his love for me, but the quality of that silence was particularly gritty and uncomfortable. There was some emotion I couldn't name, but which I later articulated as shame, perhaps humiliation. And as this feeling shifted in him, it was also mirrored in me, releasing minute spores through my system. Eventually, I stopped asking him to help me reconstruct her and took things into my own hands.

A river ran past the bottom of the bungalow's garden and in late spring and summer, if the weather conditions were right, the water turned a deep, reddish pink—a phenomenon that inspired the name, Strawberry Water.

The house was twee and anachronistic: a Colonial-style bungalow built in the 1920s, standing alone in the middle of acres of flat farmland. It had painted wooden panels on the front, wide steps leading to the front door, and even a kind of veranda, deep enough for two garden chairs. The large, open-plan living/dining room and my father's bedroom were at the front of the house, the bathroom was stuck on the side of the building, and the kitchen and my own bedroom were at the back, facing the long garden. Most of the time I couldn't see the river from my bedroom window, but I could hear it, and sometimes I could smell it. But after rain or a full moon, when the water was high, I could see the top of it, like a thin shining ribbon.

Being on the same level as the garden made the outside spaces feel like an extension of the inside. The double French doors in my room opened on to the lawn and intensified the sense that the garden and the river were somehow part of my private space. As soon as the weather was warm enough each spring, I kept my door open and spent much of my time playing outside and sitting on the river bank, or collecting leaves, flowers and stones.

In my bedroom, there was a ladder of six wooden shelves that filled the alcove beside the chimney breast on the internal wall. At my insistence, my father had painted the shelves with pastel-pink gloss. Here, in front of the books, I placed the small pebbles I'd collected over time from the banks of the river. These pale, rounded stones were the Mother Stones—each one represented a piece of information about my mother that I'd gleaned over the years:

- one stone represented my mother's name—Olivia;

- one stone represented her only daughter—me;

- one was her age when she left me—thirty-two (she was sixteen years younger than my father; I once overheard my father blame this age difference for, what he called, 'the cracks in the relationship');

- one stone was her hair colour—dark brown;

- one was for the pointed shoes I had seen in the photograph;

- one was a slim white bullet shaped stone, my personal favourite, that represented her long, thin fingers (a fact corroborated by my Aunt Francesca, who once said I had inherited her elegant hands);

- one for her occasional and unaccountable melancholia;

- one for her kindness to and love of animals.

The final two stones on the list symbolised the more abstract pieces of data that I had picked up when eavesdropping on conversations between my father and Aunt Francesca. For me, these were the most gratifying features on the list. They supported the good, rather than the callous version of the person I envisioned. They gave her humanity, a texture, and offered me an aspect of her personality I could cling to, the kind of detail a *real* relationship might offer.

I needed desperately to believe she was decent. She had left her husband and her baby daughter, but perhaps she had secret reasons.

I stuck the only photograph of my mother—the old Polaroid—on the wall and placed the stones on the shelves at different points from top to bottom, two on each glossed plank, some wide apart, some closer together, so that when I joined them with an imaginary thread, it expanded and tapered and sketched out a geometrical figure made of different sized triangles: my mother.

Every night before sleep I performed a ritual, connecting the stones in my mind's eye, dot to dot. As I touched each pebble in turn with my forefinger, I spoke the lines of information I'd learned by heart, whispered urgently like a bland and rapid liturgy, repeated three times:

Her name is Olivia,
she is thirty-two,
she has dark-brown hair,
and black shiny shoes,
and elegant hands;
she is sometimes sad,
but she loves all animals.
She is my mother.

And so, in my yearning, I conjured her. This murky, fantasy presence—held ageless in time—looked over me and became a surrogate of sorts, protective and loving, as every good mother should be.

I used to wonder whether the intent behind my ritual somehow reached my real mother, as powerful and subtle as a spell, pushing through the distant layers of subliminal connection like an ethereal pulsar. I wondered this because she came to check on me once, when I was very small.

It was summer and I was playing in the garden with my dolls. My father had let me play out past my bedtime, while he made supper in the kitchen and kept an eye on me through the kitchen window. I remember I was happy because the river water was a vivid, molten pink, reflecting the sunset in its rhythmic plaiting—a magical occurrence that only happened a few times each year. Then, something made me look up, a bird screeching and flying upwards perhaps, a twig cracking underfoot, I don't remember exactly, but there in the small copse on the other side of the river, I saw a dark figure, a woman, standing motionless in the shadows of the trees, staring at me. I remember that I felt afraid and I turned and called out to my father, but when I turned back, she was gone.

When I thought about it, years later, I had to accept the fact that she could have been anyone, any woman out for a stroll on a beautiful midsummer's evening. It was the way she stared at me, though, with such absorption and intent—she made me feel as if I meant something to her.

I continued the stone ceremony for years, and eventually it irritated me and became a chore, as necessary and tedious as cleaning my teeth. Yet I felt bound by it, anchored, as if those invisible lines that connected each stone were a web in which I placed myself. Without this structure I might plummet. Lying in bed at night, when moonlight poured through my curtainless window, I'd watch the Mother Stones—lit up bright, like bone. I often dwelt on what might happen if I stopped my ritual. Would she be lost to me forever? And, perversely, I feared that if I stopped, I might lose the control and distance I had maintained and thereby unconsciously *become* her, or at least the part of her that was unacceptable—what else might I have inherited from her along with her elegant hands? Perhaps some corrupted gene? An errant Lilith strain? For a parent to leave their child—a mother, no less!—for a mother to leave their only young daughter suggested a failing, a disorder, and the deficiency of some crucial ingredient—like the human instinct for love, or empathy.

The end of the Mother ceremony came by stealth. I was always a serious and academic child—I could have been lonely, if it weren't for the few equally geeky and self-conscious little friends I managed to make—but when I became a teenager, everything changed. Puberty altered my face and body in ways I could never have predicted, and the attention I began to receive from the opposite sex, in turn, increased my confidence. The self-reliance, eccentricity and intellect that had made me weird before, now that I was attractive, gave me allure. I became popular overnight—it was fresh and abrupt, like the sun when it emerges from cloud and alters every perception. The appearance in my life of friends and boys, alcohol and parties distracted me and went some way to filling the emptiness I'd always felt. And so, the spaces between the Mother rituals grew longer, until they fell away entirely.

I discovered, at least for that brief period, that all was well. The sadness was there, but it was less acute, lying dormant. I still thought of my lack of a mother occasionally, and I compared my experience with other's in order to gauge what I had lost—and what I had also possibly gained, given how many of my teenage friends seemed to hate their mothers. Crucially, my world had not fallen apart without the ritual. I hadn't turned into the abomination I feared I might if I released my reconstructed mother and the stones that represented her. I remember the deep relief and sense of liberation I felt when, at sixteen, on a hot summer's evening, I let the ritual go.

I was in high spirits because I'd just received my exam results, which were outstanding, and on top of that it was a strawberry-water day. I returned the Polaroid to a photo album, slipped it back between the card and the plastic on some random page; I scooped up the eight Mother Stones from the shelves in my bedroom and marched to the bottom of the garden. One by one, I threw the pebbles into the river and watched the circular ripples expanding in the pink water, dreaming about my huge future.

The time came for me to leave and go to university. I got a first-class degree in history, travelled for a couple of years, and finally settled into a research job I liked in the city, which paid me enough to cover the rent on a two-bedroom flat nearby. Throughout my twenties, I went through the usual spectrum of unstable relationships with men, but none of them lasted—until I met Michael. He was a work colleague, and we sat at opposite ends of an open-plan office for a year, but I only noticed him at a work dinner when I was seated next to him. It was his best friend's thirtieth, and he made a short speech about the love between friends, which was hilarious and touching. We were the last ones to leave the restaurant, we talked for hours, I had never felt so at home with anyone before.

We dated, fell in love, he moved into my flat, and after two years together, we married. Six months later, I was pregnant.

During the whole of my pregnancy I was unquestioningly happy—a deep contentment I had never before experienced. Even throughout my relationship with Michael, I was aware of a sense of dissociation. But during my pregnancy it abandoned me entirely. I felt connected. I felt... never alone. The continual ache of absence, like a mild grief, was replaced by the lively buzz of a constant presence, the dependant and pure vitality of a little soul, a companion, so close to me, so part of me, there was no risk of separation. The uninterrupted continuation of my baby inside my body was a source of endless joy and comfort. I could have been pregnant indefinitely. But the due date loomed. Then finally it came, and went, and ten days later, she decided to make her slow arrival.

The contractions woke me up early in the morning with the force and foreboding of an air-raid siren. Despite the shock, at first I was relieved, glad they hadn't induced me as they had been threatening to do since the due date passed. But soon, the feeling of relief was overtaken by tremendous pain and agitation, and I began to panic.

Michael drove me immediately to the hospital. My father had paid for a private room—'I don't want a repeat of what happened last time, when she was born,' I had overheard him saying to Michael in our dining room one Sunday, as I pulled the roast chicken out of the oven. This piece of information would have been like gold dust to me before, and I would have questioned him endlessly for more details of my birth, but in my blissful third trimester I didn't want any reminder of my mother to jinx this happy time.

The labour was a long and difficult one. Michael did his best—he was by my side throughout, but he might as well have not been. I felt a greater isolation than I had ever experienced, fully possessed by that primal process. In that lilac-coloured private room, midwives came and went as I paced the length of the bed, the curved fibreglass periphery of the birthing pool. I longed to get into it, to be surrounded by deep, warm water, but the midwives wouldn't allow it. If I went in too soon, it would slow the contractions. Those relentless, vice-like waves, intent on delivering

13

my baby, gripped me from the outside in and then the inside out, like a squeezed tube of paint. No one could help me. In those long hours, nature revealed her true unmodified self to me, and she was dispassionate, obdurate and brutal. I had never felt so close to the presence of death—death not as a flat, lifeless thing, but as something rowdy and muscular. I was sure that one of us would not survive. Nature's priority was to preserve life, but not necessarily mine. My life, my suffering, was totally inconsequential.

Despite their ferocity, the contractions seemed to be ineffectual and my cervix dilated remarkably slowly. At one horrifying moment, the midwife and doctor became locked in an urgent discussion, and I remember hearing the words 'anterior cervical lip' and 'foetal distress' being whispered *sotto voce* behind me. Then next to me, in a metal tray on the trolley, I saw a stainless steel medical tool, like a crochet needle, both elegant and monstrous, and I knew this tool would be used if my labour did not advance as expected.

Perhaps it was the sight of that terrifying implement that nudged me forwards—finally, after twenty-four hours of pain, I was dilated enough to be allowed to step into the warm, calming water of the birthing pool. After another forty minutes, and the brief intensity of pushing, she arrived, slipping out with one final acute twinge of pain.

A heavy peace fell like mist in the room. Shocked and silent, I watched my tiny baby as she floated under the reddening water, which glittered beneath the dimmed electric lights.

She was beautiful and otherworldly. She was still attached to me by the umbilical cord, and her tiny arms were open and waving, her dark hair swirling to and fro, like the finest grasses underwater. They pulled her up, on to my chest and I looked down into her black eyes, which stared unseeing, still full of the mysterious place she had just left behind. And while I heard my husband sobbing with joy behind me, I was overcome with a feeling of heavy solemnity, acknowledging the responsibility and duty I now carried towards this vulnerable creature.

Afterwards, following the delivery of the afterbirth, I lay in the bath in the washroom next door while Michael stayed in the lilac birthing room, holding our whimpering daughter to his bare chest. The bath water slowly turned dark as the blood was washed from my limbs, and I remember looking out over the town from the large top-floor window. It was

15

dawn and the sky was pewter-grey, with a glowing strip of red where the sun pushed up, as if congealed on the horizon. I looked at the silver metal rail of the fire escape outside the window: it was lit up red, like an arrow pointing away. In a flash vision, as clear as a film projection, I saw myself putting on a bathrobe and slippers and escaping out of that window, and down the fire escape and away from my baby and the impossible job of being a perfect mother.

In the weeks that followed, I got to grips with the many new things I had to do to care for my baby. I was relieved that the instinct to love her, deeply and unconditionally, came naturally—but nothing else did. The nappy changes and the baths, changing her tiny outfits, putting tiny, delicate arms into tiny sleeves, holding her properly, even knowing how to support her head so it didn't drop back horribly like a bowling ball in a sack, these were all skills to learn. She didn't latch on properly, so breastfeeding was agonising in the first weeks. Tears streamed down my cheeks with pain each time she sucked hungrily. With the help of the midwife I learned how to attach her correctly, and once my cracked and sore nipples healed things improved.

In the weeks after the birth I slept when she slept and cared only for my baby daughter. Michael was at work on weekdays and left us in our bubble to get on with it. Freya was thriving, despite my initial struggles with breastfeeding—now she fed on me with a sense of serious entitlement and a firmness of purpose that both alarmed and captivated me.

But in the months that followed, as Freya grew and changed, and as my love for her intensified, so did the constant dread that something would happen to her. The old feelings of grief and dismay at the loss of my mother also returned. Now that I knew first-hand what it felt like to love and care for my own child, I wondered how had my mother been able to abandon hers? What kind of a person was she? Was there something about my father that had made her leave? Was there something about me?

If I could get answers to my questions, if I could meet my mother, face-to-face, I might find solace. Resolve. In my most optimistic moments, I allowed myself the luxury of hoping I might even forge a new relationship with her, and gain the understanding I needed to forgive her past actions. By extension, I would be a better mother to my daughter than she had ever been to me.

. . .

There were ways and means of finding lost people, others managed; I had never even tried.

I visited my father first. He was now approaching eighty and he no longer lived at Strawberry Water. He'd sold it after Aunt Francesca died a few years earlier, moving into assisted living accommodation on the outskirts of town. It was over a decade since I'd even mentioned my mother to him. But he'd softened in his old age and I hoped he might now be a little more forthcoming. I explained that I was keen to trace her and asked him if he knew anything at all about her whereabouts, where might she have gone when she left? I sat opposite him in the large communal living room, in a high-backed armchair, and clutched my hands together, half expecting that old response: the uncomfortable silence, the tangible sense of opprobrium. The reaction I got was one I least expected.

'Olivia? Who's Olivia?' he asked, and I was speechless for a moment, trying to assess whether he was trying to be funny, or whether atrophy had affected his brain.

'Dad? Really?'

'That name is familiar…' he said.

'Dad! It's the name of my mother, your wife!' I said.

'My wife? I had a wife…?' He looked sky-wards as if trying to remember. 'Oh, yes. *Her!*' He shook his head, then chuckled to himself. 'Ireland, Australia, Iceland, Rome—she could be anywhere. Anywhere!' He shrugged, and looking confused again, he finished his mug of tea, placed it carefully on the table, stood stiffly and shuffled out of the room without an explanation, leaving me alone and adrift in my uncertainty.

I spoke to the manager of the housing organ-isation and she allowed me access to a folder of legal documents and passports they held for him. There was nothing at all that belonged to my mother, but I found my parents' marriage certificate, with the date and place of registration, and my mother's full name and date of birth.

I went through all the usual channels: missing persons, Baptism records, genealogy sites. I didn't get anywhere. In the end, I decided to pay for a private investigator and gave him all the information I had, including the marriage certificate. A month later, I received a phone call. My heart pumped fast and hard as told he me he'd managed to find my mother…that he was sorry to inform me that she had died…only three months before…in the house where she'd lived for the last twenty years. Where she was before that, he couldn't tell me—there was no information.

Michael was concerned when I told him. He didn't think that any good could come from me going to see the empty house where the mother I had never known had lived and died. I explained how important it was to me, to get some sort of closure. In the end, he offered to look after Freya for the day, so I could have some time there alone.

I put the address into my phone and drove up grey motorways through drizzle for four hours to find myself outside a small terraced house on a long scruffy street in a dull town in the Midlands. There was a *For Sale* sign outside.

I looked through the curtainless window, but the front room was empty—just a stained pastel carpet, and floral wallpaper, with cleaner rectangular patches where pictures had hung. I longed to know what those pictures had been, pictures she'd looked at every day for twenty years. I wondered, why had she come to live here, in such a bland and unremarkable place? Why had she chosen solitude for all these years when she could have had a family that loved her?

I felt a wave of hot fury and my fists clenched tightly—I had to use all my might to stop myself from smashing her window, because it occurred to me then that this empty house was a perfect analogy, summing up all that she had been to me in life, and all that she would continue to be in death: a deserted space, ungenerous, unresolved, disquieting, only hinting at the presence of a character. Despite my anger, I stayed, hoping to mop up some sort of sense of her, to feel a closeness to her.

An elderly neighbour appeared with a bag of groceries, stopped on her front garden path, and asked me directly, over the safety of her low brick wall, if I was planning to buy the house.

'Yes, I'm considering it,' I replied. 'Were they nice, the people who lived here before?' I added, feigning ignorance. 'I always like to know what the previous owners were like, before I make a decision. I think it can make a difference to the energy in the house,' I continued, undeterred by her blank expression. 'Not to mention the state of the carpets!'

She smiled then, and attempted a feeble chuckle. 'Just one lady lived here. Olivia.' She nodded benignly and looked away as she remembered. 'She kept the place spotless. And she was pleasant enough. Quiet, which we all want in a neighbour, don't we! Kept herself to herself, though she was kind—always gave me a Christmas card and remembered my birthday. I don't know who lived here before her.'

I nodded, trying hard to be breezy. 'Did she live here long?'

'She was here when I got here, twenty years ago. Far as I know, she lived here all that time on her own, apart from the moggy, of course. Well, I took her, in the end. She would have gone to the sanctuary, and an old cat like that, nobody would have taken her.'

'You took her cat? Is it still here?' I asked.

She laughed. 'Just about. Poor old thing. She's kidney problems and arthritis, bit like me! Olivia doted on her. I never owned a pet, but she's quite a comfort to me now.'

'I adore cats. Can I see her?' I asked, as casually as I could manage, although my heart was beating wildly, irrationally, almost as if I were about to meet my actual mother for the first time.

She hesitated. 'Well, yes, alright. I'll bring her out. I'd ask you in for a cuppa, but my house is a bit of a mess—can't manage the housework like I used to.'

She went inside and I stared at the dark opening of her front door. A smell of cooked minced beef came out in a warm waft of air. She returned a moment later with a decrepit looking tabby in her arms and beckoned me over. I went out through my mother's metal front gate and into the neighbour's front garden. The cat was content and placid in the old woman's arms, as I imagined she would have been in my mother's arms. I stroked the cat's head, looked into her mottled green eyes, marbled with age spots. She purred and slowly blinked at me.

'What's her name?' I asked.

'Persephone. But I call her Percy for short, like Olivia did.'

'How did she die, the woman who lived here?' I asked.

'Heart attack,' the old lady said, and she snapped her fingers abruptly. 'Just like that! Poor thing, she wasn't much over sixty. Best way to go, if you ask me, especially if you got no family to leave behind.'

She lowered the cat carefully on to the ground. Percy wound her skinny length through my legs in a figure of eight, pressing her weight against my calves. I bent and stroked her. I felt the bumps of her ribs, just as my mother would have done. I quickly wiped away the water that was pooling in my eyes. This was the closest I had ever been to her. This ancient, limping feline had orbited my mother for years. She'd sat on my mother's lap, had curled up on her warm flesh as she watched the TV. She'd been fed by her, cared for and loved by her, for years. It was so much more than I'd ever had from her.

'Persephone,' I said, and wondered at the name.

'Ooh, she really likes you,' the old woman said. 'She's not normally like this with anyone new.'

'Really?' I said, wanting to believe her. I wondered whether my smell was like my mother's, or the sound of my voice.

There were more questions I wanted to ask, about my mother, about her habits, her appearance, whether she worked. But I couldn't bring myself to admit I was Olivia's daughter—the old woman would have had too many questions of her own, questions that I couldn't answer. Or didn't want to.

. . .

I cried on and off during the drive home, with that same unresolved grief grating at my centre. When I returned to our flat that evening, I found Michael and Freya snuggled up under a duvet on the sofa, eating jam on toast and watching a programme about deep-sea creatures.

Freya beamed up at me and waved her piece of sucked toast in the air. 'Mamamamamamama,' she repeated, saying my name for the first time.

My heart burst like a firework in a dark sky. Why was I chasing an idea of a dead person, who in life had never shown me devotion or affection, when I had these two real living souls to love, who also loved and needed me?

Then, a month later, Strawberry Water came up for sale. Michael always checked the house prices in the rural areas of the county that were still within commuting distance of the city. We both dreamed of escaping the clamour and finding somewhere bucolic to bring up Freya. Most of the time the asking price was prohibitive. Michael pointed it out to me on the estate agent's webpage, commenting on its low price in relation to its size. I recognised it immediately.

We went for a viewing, at first simply out of curiosity. I had forgotten what an odd yet charming bungalow it was, set in open farmland with the river running by at the bottom of the long garden, and it had been pleasantly refurbished and spruced up. We wandered from one cold empty room to another. Perhaps it was merely the lack of furniture and home comforts, but despite its tasteful interiors, I couldn't shake the feeling that the house didn't want me there.

The agent showed us around and explained that the price was low because the people who lived there were keen to secure a quick sale, though he couldn't elaborate.

Michael loved it. Principally, he loved the price. I told him that I had my reservations, that my relationship with it should remain in the past and to return might tempt some sort of unhappy fate. He laughed and hugged me. He thought I was being superstitious, paranoid, that it might be the only opportunity we would have for many years to buy a detached home where Freya could have her own room.

'And the river!' he said with delight.

In the end, he convinced me that we should put

in an even lower offer than the asking price and leave the decision to providence.

Secretly, I was confident our offer would be declined.

It wasn't.

The day we moved in, I went straight to my old bedroom at the back of the house and was flooded with memories and nostalgia. The shelves in the chimneybreast were still there, empty and sparkling with new, white gloss paint. I would fill them with children's books, and wooden toys—it would be little Freya's nursery.

Looking out of the French doors, down the long garden to the river, I could see the water level was high—a twisting braid of water was just visible. It was a view that was acutely familiar, so intimate that it was as if it was perfectly mirrored inside me. I knew it all, from the shape of the lawn and its slight camber, to the forms of light and shadow in the spaces between the trees on the other side of the river.

I wandered to the bottom of the garden. The river was brown, rushing by and swollen from a recent storm. Breathing in, that familiar smell of damp and acrid foliage evoked the past. Then, for old time's sake, I collected some pretty pebbles from the riverbank and put them in my pocket.

Turning back towards the house, my heart lunged: I saw Freya, unaccompanied and staggering down the lawn towards me. She'd recently learned to walk and was keen to go everywhere on foot. She was gurgling little shouts of delight as she spotted the river and increased her step, heading towards the bank. I trotted to her and scooped her up, returning to the house. Michael was in the kitchen unpacking crockery.

'What are you doing letting her come out here on her own? She could drown in that river—she was heading straight for it!'

He turned to me and looked surprised. 'She was in her car seat fast asleep,' he said. 'How did she get out, was she not belted in? You're the one who carried her in from the car.'

The empty car seat was on the floor in the middle of the living room, the undone straps with their plastic buckles hanging loose over either side.

'I thought I had…I was sure I had,' I said. 'Don't look at me like that! You should have put those child gates up on the back doors before you did anything else.'

He tutted and turned away from me, with a certain look of disdain that cut me to the quick—it was an expression I had never seen on his face before. I carried Freya into my old room and placed the pebbles on the shelves, this time in a simple straight line across the top shelf, out of Freya's reach: an homage to my mother, as well as a sign to myself that I was free from her.

Holding Freya by the French doors, she pointed at the dozens of rooks flying across the sky. 'Barrrdee, barrdee, barrdee,' she called out in gentle repetitions, between the harsh sounds of their caw-cawing.

In the woods on the other side of the river, I looked at the grey collection of shapes between the black silhouettes of the trees and I thought I saw a dark form flitting chaotically between them. No doubt a fox or a deer, but it sent an unpleasant shiver through me.

We'd been in the house for three weeks when I invited my father round for Sunday lunch. He'd recently suffered a nasty bout of flu, and as he'd just turned eighty, I felt an urgent need to spend more time with him. I thought seeing the old place again would cheer him up.

But just after I got off the phone with him, Michael said he didn't feel like entertaining, that having my father over tomorrow couldn't be worse timing. He'd just returned from his usual Saturday bike ride, and he was sweaty, red-faced and mud-splattered. It had been raining all day. He complained that he was overtired—it had been a particularly stressful week at work, the daily commute was longer, and he'd been woken every night by Freya's crying. He wanted to spend Sunday snoozing on the sofa in front of the TV, he said.

I had little sympathy. I'd been stuck in the house with Freya all day and she'd been fractious— I hadn't been able to placate her. And I noticed he hadn't been tired enough to cancel his cycling with 'the boys'—apparently, he needed to explore the new neighbourhood. But on top of that, he wasn't the one doing the night feeds.

Freya had never slept through the night, but since we moved into the house her sleep was even more disturbed. The health visitor said thirteen months was a very respectable age to stop breast feeding and so, following her advice I had begun weaning her. I'd hoped her sleep would improve with the more substantial bottle feeds, but she didn't take well to it. Whether her restlessness was down to the new environment, or the change from breast to cow's milk, I wasn't sure, but since the day we'd moved to Strawberry Water she woke repeatedly throughout the night. I hadn't wanted to stop breastfeeding—it felt like another small separation between us—but I was driven by a desperate need for rest, and I assumed that at least with a bottle Michael would be able to take over sometimes. So far, my expectation had not been met.

'I don't see why you should be so tired, you're not the one getting up to do the feeds!' I said, as he complained.

'I still get woken up, you know. And I'm at work all day.'

'So am I! *This* is work. This is the hardest work I've ever done. And you know, it's funny how you seem to be fast asleep whenever I ask you to get up and help me.'

'I can't nap in the day like you do.'

'You think I nap? How do you think the cleaning and washing and cooking get done?'

When my father arrived the next day, Michael snoozed on the sofa while Freya napped in the nursery. As the chicken roasted, we sat in the dining room and looked through an old photograph album my father had brought over. There were snapshots of me as a toddler on the lawn in front of the house, a couple of me in a playpen by the river in summer, and one of me and my father in the living room with plastic bricks on the carpet. We pointed out details and discussed what had been changed in the house and what had stayed the same. Then I came across the Polaroid photograph, the one with my mother in the dark doorway and my father and I on the steps in front of the house. The sight of it threw me back to my childhood and the days of my ritual.

'Oh, look,' I said, and passed the Polaroid to him, thrilled that a photograph with my mother, however hazily captured, had made it through the net of my father's censorship. He studied it impartially for a while and noted only that the three wooden steps were no longer here, that they'd been replaced with brick.

'They would have rotted in the rain,' he said, and then, looking closer, 'Who is that?' He pointed with a shaky finger to the figure in the doorway.

'It's Olivia,' I said.

His eyes whipped up at me and then back at the photograph. 'No, no, no,' he said.

I assumed that, like the last time, he'd forgotten who she was. 'Olivia—remember, Dad, your wife? My mother?'

'Yes, I know who you mean. It's not her. It can't be,' he said. 'You're wearing the yellow dress we bought for your christening. I remember that dress. It must be Aunt Francesca.'

'No, because Aunt Francesca told me she took the photograph,' I said. 'It must be Olivia.'

I continued to look through the rest of the photographs, ignoring him—he was clearly confused.

But, still looking closely at the photograph held in his shaking hand, he went on, 'You were christened in that dress at sixteen months old.' He was smiling to himself at the recollection. 'I can remember that dress, with broderie anglaise across the front. Such a bright yellow,' he said. He took my hand and looked at me. 'But *she* had already gone by then. When you were only thirteen months old. So who that woman there is, God only knows!'

I searched his face for clarity, his grey eyes were mournful.

Then Freya broke the silence with a scream and I jumped from my chair and rushed to her.

. . .

33

After dinner I drove my father home. When I returned, I noticed that he'd left the photograph album behind, lying open on the dining room table. I checked on Freya in the nursery, she was sleeping peacefully. It wouldn't last. There was a plastic magnifying glass in her toy box and I tugged it out, slowly and gently from beneath a pile of toys. I froze when Freya gurgled and fidgeted, but to my relief she didn't wake up.

Settling in the kitchen, I studied the Polaroid photograph through the magnifying glass. The misty figure in the internal door was merely a shadow, an impression of a person—the long, pale fingers that clutched around the door, fingers that for so many years I believed belonged to my mother, were blurred and out of focus. I looked at the shoe that protruded at the bottom of the doorframe— pointed, shiny, old-fashioned. It could be anyone. With a feeling of hollowness, I let the photograph fall from my fingers and I opened the French doors, stepping over the child gates Michael had finally installed.

It was dusk now and the sky was clear, the air was fragrant and refreshed after the days of rain we'd recently had. The sun was diminishing through a mass of low clouds, tinted green and lilac on the horizon. In the other half of the sky, a bright half-moon was shining out, suspended in deepest indigo. I stood by the river, my feet sinking into the soft grassy bank. There were large encircling ovals of oily pink and blue moving on the surface of the water like Italian marble. I remembered the woman I'd seen that day as a child, who'd stood and stared at me while I played with my dolls on the lawn, and I looked up at the dark trees on the other side of the river to the space where she'd been. There was a path that ran parallel to the river and then led through the trees and into a meadow on the other side. This must have been where she'd come from. But who was she? Was she my mother? I thought of the woman in the Polaroid photograph. Was *she* my mother? With my father's mind deteriorating as it was, it was impossible to know the truth. Then for some reason, an image of myself during Freya's birth flashed up in my mind, and I thought of the woman I had become, the shambolic and feral female who growled and shouted and paced that room. It was a part of me that was unrecognisable, a part that I couldn't quantify or now connect with. All these women—who were they? I would never be sure.

My gaze lingered on the glossy grey mud of the river wall on the opposite bank. I noticed that the roots of a tree bulged out of the muddy flank. Some of the roots curved back into the bank and some of them opened out straight into the water, like frayed, loose wires, with no earth to grip on to. I watched the water as it curled around the roots and tugged at them softly, endlessly.

I barely slept that night. Freya kept waking up and crying and I wasn't able to drop off between her cries because I kept hearing a strange noise, like a grinding and rolling, which intensified and receded in waves. In the morning, I asked Michael if he'd heard anything. He said he hadn't. 'Probably that ancient boiler,' he suggested.

The following three nights saw no improvement. Freya woke every few hours, and although I offered her the bottle, she seemed uninterested. The mysterious grinding and rolling noise persisted, as if it had worked its way under my skin.

I tried to nudge Michael awake. 'You go. You go this time, *please*. I *have* to sleep,' I begged, pushing and rocking his stodgy body.

He just grunted and rolled over.

I couldn't bear to lie there and hear my baby screaming without going to her, though I longed to rest, just for an hour or two—it was a desire for sleep as intense as the famished might hunger for food, or the drowning might crave for a gulp of sweet air.

I sat in the nursery on the rocking chair with Freya on my lap and gave her the bottle. She fed painfully slowly, taking her time. She seemed happy now, as if nothing had happened, and annoyingly, was wide awake. Every now and then, she stopped, detaching from the teat with a pop and smiling up at me, her amber eyes aglow. If I hadn't known better, I would have said there was mischief or devilment in her expression.

I switched off the night light to calm her and then noticed the moonlight coming in through the curtainless French doors, resting flatly across the furniture in the room. I felt a torrent of despondency and gloom wash over me. The sound of two owls, one calling and one answering, again and again, made me drowsy and I fell asleep. In my dream, the rolling noise intensified: a gritty, whirring and grinding sound like a stone being rolled back and forth over a hard surface. It seemed to make its way to the heart of me, as if the noise were a movement that was occurring at my very centre.

I woke with a start, and my dread was replaced with panic as I sensed the cold emptiness on my lap. Where was Freya?

The unearthly moonlight and an almost-tangible coldness filled the room. I looked down to the floor, and turned around frantically, and then I noticed her little body through the bars of the cot, snuggled up and fast asleep under her blanket. But how had she got there? I had no memory of moving her. I stood, turned on the main light and looked over the side of the cot at her—she seemed peaceful enough. But then I noticed a strange mark on her little wrist, like two oval smudges of lilac paint, like finger prints. I licked my finger and tried to gently to wipe them off, but it wasn't paint, they were bruises. Freya moaned and turned over in her sleep and so I left her alone.

The next day I was nauseous and groggy. Freya and I snoozed on and off until the afternoon, curled up in my king-size bed. My usual routine went awry. When Michael came home, he told me I looked awful, then said he would order a takeaway because I hadn't made dinner.

The following day, I put Freya in her cot for her afternoon sleep. She slept for an uncharacteristically long time—I even managed to wash-up, prepare a soup and snatch a half an hour snooze. Then, after three or four hours, I heard the rolling noise again. I usually only heard it at night—this was a new development. It seemed to be coming from inside the wall of the nursery. It was an aggressive and urgent rolling and grinding, and it terrified me.

I found Freya still sleeping peacefully in her cot. But the room was cold and oppressive, like an old church, or an outdoor building, and it smelled damp, like river water.

A surge of fury rose up in me. I unlocked and shoved open all the windows. I bent over the cot and picked Freya up brusquely. More brusquely than I had intended. It was time for her feed, and she needed changing; if she slept any longer, she'd be up all night. The thought of another sleep-deprived night filled me with dread. She screamed with outrage at such a rude awakening, and as her cries cut though me, I turned towards the door and saw that the stones on the shelves had been moved. They were no longer in the straight line on the top shelf, where I had put them, but placed across the shelving at different points, in a pattern I recognised, a pattern I knew by heart. It was the Mother shape.

I felt sick. I collected all the stones together and put them in Freya's toy bucket. Holding her in my arms, I stormed through the house to the garden. Freya had stopped crying, distracted by all the action. I plonked her down on the grass, where she sat and resumed her bawling, barefaced to the heavens, while I went to the edge of the water and hurled the stones into the churning river.

'Did you move the stones on the shelves in the nursery?' I asked Michael, that evening.

'What stones?' he replied.

As the week drew on, I became gradually more fretful. I wasn't sure whether it was exhaustion or because I'd stopped breastfeeding, but I felt increasingly disconnected from Freya.

I spent more and more time in my bedroom because there was something else that bothered me: I had begun to feel ill at ease and vulnerable when I went about the house. Moving from room to room, there was a coldness that followed me; I could feel it at the back of my neck, a feeling of vulnerability and exposure, as if something was about to envelop me.

In order to get away, I went to visit my father one evening.

'Why did she go? Was it me?' I asked with a boldness, an entitlement I had never dared express before.

He was quiet for a moment, then his eyes lit up as he recalled something. 'Well, she talked about the birds a lot. She kept talking about birds. She told me a story once about birds and eggs, about how when she was a little girl, she'd touched a blackbird's eggs in the nest and then the blackbird had never returned. It left its own babies to perish. She'd tried to incubate the baby birds, but they all died. Humans must never touch a bird's egg, because the bird will sense the presence of the 'other' and reject their own.'

Losing patience, I stood up and shouted at him, 'What the hell are you going on about?'

He looked up at me and cowered, as if afraid, and I saw how vulnerable and confused he had become.

I sat down, sickened by my behaviour, and held his hand. 'I'm sorry, Dad,' I said. 'I'm sorry...'

There was a storm that night. The howling wind rose and diminished in time with Freya's cries, and between the gale I still heard the terrible rolling and grinding noise, louder than ever. I left Freya to cry and I went to the kitchen and stared out of the French doors. The bushes and trees were being battered, pulled this way and that as if they were made from flimsy material. The river was so high that I could see it from where I stood. It was a strange dark red. I took four sleeping pills and returned to bed. I held the pillow tightly over my head and waited for sleep to come.

The next morning, I asked Michael if he had heard the dreadful sounds in the night, the rolling and grinding.

'If you mean your daughter crying, then yes, I heard that loud and clear. I had to get up to see to her four times in the night.

He left for work without saying goodbye and I fell back to sleep.

When I awoke, I looked out of the window. The storm had passed and the sky was clear and blue. I felt refreshed and buoyant. I looked at the clock. I had slept for four consecutive hours for the first time in over a year.

I went straight into the nursery, perplexed as to why Freya had slept so late. I found her wide awake and standing up in her cot, smiling and giggling. I approached her with my arms outstretched, but she shook her head vigorously and backed away, saying, 'Lyday, lyday lydadylydaylyday. No, Mama! No, Mamamamama. Lyday! Lyday!' She pointed towards the door, half laughing and half crying now, confused by her own emotions.

'What do you want, darling?' I asked, reaching again for her.

But she shook her head and pushed me away, repeating, now with more volume and urgency, as if desperate for me to understand, 'Layday, lydaylydaylydaylydaylydaylydaylydaylyday!' She became red in the face and irate.

Exasperated, I tried to grab her, to lift her out of her cot, but she struggled out of my hands. I stormed out of the room, and slammed the door, shouting in an ugly voice, 'Be like that, then—if you want to be mean to Mummy, go ahead!'

That night, once Freya was bathed and asleep in her cot, I asked Michael, 'Who's the lady?'

'What?' he said, looking up from his laptop— he was working at the dining room table, his dirty dinner plate pushed to one side.

'Have you had someone over here, or something? Freya keeps asking for a 'Lady' like she wants someone, but it isn't me.'

Michael looked at me wearily for a long moment, then said, 'You think I have the energy for that? Don't you think the lady might be you? Don't you think she might want her mummy back, just like I'd like my wife back?'

'What do you mean?'

He rubbed his brow as he turned back to his work, no offer of an explanation.

I wasn't sure what had woken me, I was aware only of the sense that time had passed—nothing else. I felt unreal, woolly. Like post-anaesthesia. I had taken sleeping pills again and they had made me groggy and unnerved. Each crease in the thin sheet that stretched over me was suddenly brought to my attention, irritating the hairs on my skin. There was a mauve light coming into the room in folds at the top of the curtains. Michael was snoring gently next to me, the sound of paper tearing.

I pulled myself from bed and wandered slowly through the house. That same odd feeling seemed to blanket the spaces I moved through, a

cold sensation. I felt foreign in my own territory. I
found myself gently pulling open the kitchen door,
listening to the slow and familiar click as the handle
turned. The garden possessed a heavy humidity,
but I could also feel the cool moisture that would
soon jewel the grass with dew. In the pre-dawn half-
light, I made my way towards the bottom of the
garden and stopped by the river. I felt light-headed
and lowered myself to the ground. I sat in my
nightdress on the riverbank, feeling the hard earth
and the prickle of grass beneath me. The water
was dark and shifting thickly southwards, where I
knew it would eventually join the sea, some twenty
miles away. I watched the half-moon's reduced,
trembling reflection in the bluish black, spreading
and contracting. Then, as time passed, the sun rose
and little strips of water went pink, like streaming
ribbons appearing on the surface and disappearing.
As I tried to pin down these elusive pink ribbons
with my gaze, another form came into shape,
beneath the water, like a small, pale mammal,
moving and bobbing. I inched down the bank to
see it more clearly, and to my horror the shape of
a baby came into focus, the body of a baby, or a
small child, submerged and helpless. A low, guttural

sound came out of me, and then I recognised the face of my own daughter. I screamed, and called out her name. She was underwater on her back, looking up towards me, her eyes bright and amber, her hair swirling like silken grasses. I let myself slip down the bank and flopped heavily into the water. I sank swiftly down, grasping hysterically at the little body with both of my hands, hammering at the water again, and again.

There was nothing there. There was nothing.

I stopped and I stood up, and found myself waist-deep in water. My heart was racing. I let it slow as my panic began to subside. I felt the embrace of the muddy riverbed, soft clay, enclose my feet and ankles. The water was without temperature, as if it were the same warmth as my blood. The current shifted weightily around my body, like oil, slightly tugging me one way and then the other, and as it did it seemed to pull something jagged out from inside me, until I felt extraordinarily smooth and peaceful. I could smell the scent of rich earth and the summer foliage, brought through on a sultry breeze that rippled through the trees. A silvery peel of birdsong started up, so sweet and lazy, reminiscent of something good and nostalgic, like a longing for something that you could almost reach if you just kept listening. I listened, and listened. And as I listened, my gaze fell on the path that wound through the copse on the other side of the river. Where the woods ended, the path crossed a wide, dry meadow and continued through the grasses, dividing the field diagonally. In the far distance, on the other side of the meadow, I could see a stile. I wondered how easy it would be to swim across the river and follow that path to wherever it led.

I looked back at the house, squat and rigid, and possessed, at the other end of the garden. Freya would be waking soon. But I didn't want to leave this feeling, this peacefulness, this homeliness.

And what good was I to them, now?

I took a few steps towards the middle of the river. It got only fractionally deeper, reaching my chest. The strawberry-pink patina undulated on the yellow cotton of my nightdress. I thought it was strange that this was the first time in my life I had actually been in the river, even though it had been here all these years. Now I was in it, it was so easy, so natural. I studied the bank on the other side, where the path began. It was steep and muddy, but where the tree roots bulged out from the river wall, there were three possible footholds.

If I was quick, I could swim across the river and follow the path that led through the wood and across the meadow, before the sun fully rose.

Acknowledgements

I am deeply grateful to Matt Freidson, Deputy Director at Creative Future, for his generosity, encouragement and tireless behind-the-scenes commitment to supporting talented, under-represented writers who might not otherwise get noticed. Huge thanks also to Creative Future, New Writing South and Myriad for giving me this opportunity. I am grateful to my wonderful writing mentor, Erinna Mettler, for her patient and expert guidance, and for shining a light on my blind spots. Also, to Victoria Heath Silk for ironing out any remaining creases with her excellent editing skills. I am so grateful to my children, to Noah for his belief in me and unremitting encouragement, and to Lois, who listened attentively when I got stuck over plot points, and inspired me with her brilliant teenage brain.

About the author

Tara Gould studied visual arts at the University of Brighton and an MA at Sussex University. Her short stories have been published in anthologies including the *Asham Anthology for Women Writers*, and her plays have been broadcast on BBC Radio 4. In 2016, she was Writer In Residence at Creative Future. She lives in East Sussex.

About Spotlight

Spotlight Books is a collaboration between Myriad Editions, Creative Future and New Writing South to discover, guide and support writers whose voices are under-represented.

Our aim is to spotlight new talent that otherwise would not be recognised, and to help writers who face barriers, or lack opportunities, to develop their creative and professional skills in order to create a lasting legacy of work.

Each of our three organisations is dedicated to specific aspects of writer development. Together we are able to offer a clear ladder of support, from mentorship through to development editing and promotional opportunities.

Spotlight books are not only treasures in themselves but also beacons to other under-represented writers. For further information, please visit: www.creativefuture.org.uk

Spotlight is supported by Arts Council England.

'These works are both nourishing and inspiring,
and a gift to any reader.'—Kerry Hudson

Spotlight stories

Georgina Aboud
Cora Vincent

Tara Gould
The Haunting of Strawberry Water

Ana Tewson-Božić
Crumbs

Spotlight poetry

Jacqueline Haskell
Stroking Cerberus: Poems from the Afterlife

Elizabeth Ridout
Summon

Sarah Windebank
Memories of a Swedish Grandmother